MARLON McDOOGLE'S
MAGICAL NIGHT

Written by
SEAN COVEL

Illustrated by
DIEGO VELASQUEZ

A Gift Worth For Wishing

Chapter 1
A Gift Worth Wishing For

On an icy cold Christmas Eve not so long ago, Marlon McDoogle looked out from the window of his warm house down a long and winding road.

The sun had set some time ago, and Marlon was getting sleepy.

Twice he had nodded off, and twice he had woken up with his nose pressed against the freezing glass.

His eyes searched the snowy mountain passes for any sign of Grandpa McDoogle's old truck, but he saw only a blizzard that was just getting started.

Grandpa McDoogle always told Marlon in his thick Scottish voice, "Listen, lad. Your 12th Christmas Eve will be the finest of all. I will be bringing you a gift that you will never forget."

For as long as he could remember, Marlon wanted only one thing for Christmas: a model toy train with lots of track.

He dreamed of it every Christmas Eve, but as Christmas after Christmas passed, Marlon didn't receive the one gift he wanted most.

"Maybe tonight," Marlon whispered as he looked up the road.

Deep in the distance, almost hidden by snowflakes, he could see the faces of Mount Rushmore looking back at him.

Marlon had seen those stone faces 100 times before. But tonight, Marlon thought, they looked particularly excited.

Suddenly, headlights rounded the corner, and Grandpa McDoogle's truck rambled up the road.

In the back of the truck was a long package wrapped in gold foil with a bright red ribbon tied around it.

"That's it!" Marlon blurted. "The only thing that would need such a long box is a train set with lots of track!"

Marlon threw open the door and was blown back by a blast of snow.

There stood Grandpa McDoogle holding the present. It was almost as long as Marlon was tall.

"Marlon!" he exclaimed. "Have I got something special for you, my boy! Prepare to be amazed!"

I'm ready! Marlon thought to himself. *And I know exactly what it is!*

"Can I open it?!" Marlon asked.

With barely a nod from Grandpa McDoogle, Marlon tackled the gift to the floor, ripped off the bow, and tossed paper in every direction.

He threw the lid off of the box, and there it lay right before his eyes...

...A long, red scarf.

Marlon felt his heart drop as his mind went blank.

"Speechless with wonderment, I see!" said Grandpa McDoogle. "I knew you'd like it! Most folks might not recognize that such a simple thing can hold a world of adventure!"

Marlon wrinkled his nose as he lifted the long red scarf from the box.

Grandpa McDoogle carefully draped the scarf around Marlon's neck and gently folded it into a knot. "There." he said. "Looks perfect!"

After admiring his work for a moment, Grandpa McDoogle shot toward the door.

He pulled Marlon's coat off the hook and tossed it to him.

"Jump into your boots, lad, and throw on your coat. We have lots of work to do!"

Marlon wandered toward the door, still in shock at the present he'd just received.

An Unexpected Guest

Chapter 2
An Unexpected Guest

A lousy scarf," Marlon mumbled as Grandpa McDoogle's truck rambled down the road. "Anything would be better than a lousy scarf."

The long, thin (lousy) scarf had the outline of a steam train stitched into the end. It was just like the scarf Grandpa McDoogle had worn on the trains for the last 40 years . . . but a lot less ragged and dirty.

"Wait," Marlon suddenly realized, "Grandpa, are you taking me to work?"

"Aye. Big night!" Grandpa McDoogle gruffed. "We need all the help we can get!"

"But Grandpa," Marlon argued, "I'm 12 years old. I don't know how to work at a train station. I'm just a kid!"

"Well," Grandpa McDoogle replied, "being just a kid is your choice to make, isn't it Marlon?

"After all, I'd be nothing more than a crazy old Scotsman in a rickety old truck... if that's all I wanted to be.

"But, I choose to be something more."

Nobody really knew which side of the family Grandpa McDoogle was from, but everyone agreed that it had to be the 'strange' side.

The truck wound its way through the Black Hills of South Dakota toward Hill City.

Marlon looked from the truck as it passed the base of Mount Rushmore.

Marlon had seen those stone faces 100 times before. But this time, he thought, they looked particularly disappointed.

As Marlon and Grandpa McDoogle pulled into Hill City, the wind picked up and the blizzard blew even harder.

Marlon could barely see the station of The 1880's Train down the hill ahead.

The old truck came to a stop.

"Snug up that scarf, lad," Grandpa McDoogle said as he opened the door of his old truck. "There's big work to do and not much time to do it!"

Marlon opened his door and stepped out into the freezing night, uncertain of what was ahead.

The train yard was clamoring with activity.

Engineers, Conductors and Foremen were dashing in every direction. Each one was covered in more coal dust than the one before.

Marlon noticed that each person was wearing the same scarf that he had around his neck.

"Evening, Angus," the Conductor called out while swinging his gold watch. "Just in time!"

The roundhouse doors slid open, and a wall of steam rolled into the night.

Through the steam, Marlon could see the Number 7 locomotive chugging and banging as it pulled slowly onto the tracks.

"Grandpa, are we going to ride on the train?" Marlon asked.

"Are we going to ride on it?" said Grandpa McDoogle. "Why Marlon, I'm the Engineer. We're DRIVING it!"

Marlon's eyes widened in surprise.

This night is improving, Marlon thought.

Then a question crossed his mind.

But who takes a train on Christmas Eve? Isn't everyone at home waiting for Santa?

The wind whipped and a swoosh of snowflakes blew toward Marlon's face.

He closed his eyes, and waited for the cold blast.

But it did not come.

Marlon opened his eyes..

The wind had stopped blowing.

The clock on the round house had ticked its last tock.

And snowflakes hung motionless in the air.

Marlon heard the sound of bells
ringing in the distance.

Grandpa McDoogle turned to look
at him.

"I'd like to introduce you to a friend of
mine," Grandpa McDoogle said with
a wink.

Suddenly, Grandpa McDoogle called
out across the train station, "HE'S
COMING IN!!"

"Right on time," the Conductor called back.

Grandpa McDoogle bellowed, "Quickly, lads and lasses! Pull 'er back and light the way!"

Everyone ran to the center of the train yard where a massive mound sat covered in an old canvas tarp.

Workers scrambled to pull back the heavy tarp.

As they did, a golden glow poured out from underneath.

"MARLON!" Grandpa McDoogle shouted. "A little help!"

Marlon jumped to attention and began helping to pull the tarp back, revealing a giant round bale of hay.

The hay glowed and sparkled like it was spun from golden stars.

Marlon watched the Yard Foreman unroll hay in a long and glowing line.

A shiver of excitement turned to a shiver of cold as Marlon took a deep breath of icy air.

Grandpa McDoogle took notice and grabbed a handful of the sparkling hay.

"Let me show you a trick of the trade," he said, handing the hay to Marlon. "We pack a nip of this golden hay in our pockets. Just a wee bit will warm you up from the tip of your nose to the tips of your toes!"

The moment Marlon touched the golden hay, he warmed right up and his heart began to race.

The sound of bells grew louder and louder as a sleigh raced down from the sky.

It slid to a stop on the long strip of glowing hay.

"Grandpa... Is that really...?"

Before Marlon could finish, a deep and jolly voice came booming through the night.

"Merry Christmas to one and all!"

Santa Claus had arrived.

Santa stepped down from his sleigh
and looked to Grandpa McDoogle
with a gleam in his eye.

"Why, Angus McDoogle!
My dear great good friend.
Your grandson is with us?
What a marvelous trend.

He seems a bit young though,
Wouldn't you say?
By the time you first joined us,
Your hair was quite gray."

Santa looked to Marlon, expecting
a reply.

Marlon's mind raced with questions,
but only a few words came out.

"Whuuuuuh. . . What are you doing
here, Mr. Claus?" Marlon asked. "It's
Christmas Eve. Aren't you supposed to
be delivering presents?"

"Why, Marlon, I am," Santa replied
as he pulled a huge bag of presents
from his sleigh.

"Through London and Paris
And New York we rode.
But the reindeer are hungry
And there's much more to go.

"My belly's filled with cookies.
They'll fill theirs with hay.
And with the help of this train,
We'll be done before day!"

Santa charged toward the train as
Marlon watched the reindeer eat
the sparkling hay.

"I don't understand," Marlon said.

"Well, Marlon," Grandpa McDoogle replied, "Santa travels across the entire world delivering presents. That's tiring work. So, he stokes his fire with all the milk and cookies that folks leave for him along the way.

"But the reindeer have to work just as hard pulling a sleigh full of presents, and Santa isn't exactly a wee lad, if you catch my meaning."

"Hill City is right in the middle of Santa's route around the world, so he stops here to let the reindeer fill up on the golden hay," Grandpa McDoogle explained.

"This hay has a magic to it, my boy. It lets the reindeer ride through the sky just as easily as charging across a snowy field."

Marlon watched the reindeer in wonder.

What would it be like to race through the sky each Christmas Eve? Marlon thought.

29

Santa walked through the train yard, and everyone gathered to respectfully greet him.

Some removed their hats.

Others gave a salute.

And the ladies gave a slight curtsy.

Santa called out to each person by name.

"Misters Pemberton, Mills,
Harlan and Moon!
Misters Wagner and Phillips
And Harold the Goon!

"Young Jarvis, Old Charlie,
And Missus McGreeve!
Good to see you, my friends!
Are we ready to leave?"

Grandpa McDoogle boarded the train and quickly set to work pulling levers, turning valves, and stoking the boiler's fire. Marlon was close behind.

"MARLON!" Grandpa McDoogle hollered as he pointed to a rusty chain hanging from the ceiling, "Give that chain two long tugs to let everyone know we are rolling out!"

Marlon grabbed the dirty wooden handle and pulled the chain.

The train whistle blasted into the night.

He pulled it a second time, and the train began tugging and chugging toward the valley ahead.

Santa climbed aboard the locomotive and snapped his fingers.

His clothes transformed into overalls and an Engineer's cap.

A long red scarf with special stitching hung down from his neck.

As the train approached the first house in the valley, Marlon was struck with a thought.

"Pardon me, Mr. Claus, but how can you deliver presents from a train?" he asked.

Santa pointed to the chimney of the
first house ahead.

"I'll go up the train's smokestack,
And down into there.
I'll be swift and silent,
So no one's aware.

"I will fly house to house
As we wind through the hills.
Then back to the train
When the stockings are filled."

Santa put a finger to the edge of his
nose and vanished up the smokestack
in a cloud of magic.

A Job to Do

For
Santa

Chapter 3
A Job to Do

he magical cloud wisped across the valley and down into the chimney of the first house.

Marlon watched as the living room window glowed a warm glow.

The magical cloud whirled from the first chimney and down into the next.

The windows glowed once again.

The magical cloud quickly jumped from chimney to chimney all the way up the valley and ahead of the train.

"He's getting ahead of us!" Grandpa McDoogle shouted. "Stoke the fire as fast as you can, boy!"

Marlon shoveled more coal into the firebox and the train sped up.

"That's better!" Grandpa McDoogle hollered, "But we're still not going fast enough! GIVE IT ALL YA GOT!"

Marlon shoveled as fast as he could, but the train barely changed speed.

Then an idea popped into his head.

Marlon reached into his pocket and pulled out the magic hay.

He gripped the hay tightly for a moment, held his breath, and then tossed it into the firebox.

The train immediately began to shake and shudder.

"What in the Bonnie Boggin is that?" yelled Grandpa McDoogle.

One moment later, he had his answer.

A blast of golden steam shot from the smokestack.

But instead of billowing up into the night, the golden steam swirled down and gathered beneath the wheels.

With a loud rumble, it lifted the train up off of the tracks and into the air.

"AAAHHHRRGGGHH!!!" Grandpa McDoogle hollered.

"I've seen every place that a train can go, and up in the air is definitely not one of them!"

The Number 7 lifted higher and higher into the night sky.

Marlon saw the tracks get smaller and smaller below.

"What should we do, Grandpa?!?" Marlon shouted.

"I do not know!" Grandpa McDoogle yelled back.

"But in moments like this, doing something is always better than doing nothing!"

The train tilted sharply and tossed Marlon across the cabin.

He grabbed a lever to catch himself, and the lever moved back.

As it did, a blast of golden steam shot from the boiler.

The train creaked a loud creak and dove straight toward the ground.

"DIFFERENT!" Grandpa McDoogle yelled, "BUT NOT BETTER!"

Marlon threw the lever back, and the Number 7 pulled up from its dive, smashing through ole Mr. Warder's barn on its way back into the sky.

The locomotive banked a hard turn
and flew straight toward the faces of
Mount Rushmore.

Marlon had seen those stone faces
100 times before. But this time,
he thought, they looked
particularly surprised.

"How are we going to get this big iron beast under control!?" Grandpa yelled.

Marlon thought as hard as he could think.

He scrunched his eyebrows so tight that an idea popped out.

Then he went to work, taking a chance.

Marlon pulled off his scarf.

He lashed it around levers and spun it around spinners.

He wound it around gauges and pulled it across pulleys.

Soon, every control in the train was tied up in Marlon's long red scarf.

"Marlon!" Grandpa McDoogle yelled. "We're trying to drive this train, not keep it warm!"

"In moments like this, doing something is always better than doing nothing, right Grandpa?" said Marlon as he gripped the scarf tight and planted his feet solidly on the floor.

Marlon pulled the scarf to the right and the levers leaned in.

He pulled the scarf to the left and the wheels whirled closed.

Steam spurted wildly with each and every pull.

The train swung wide to the left and wide to the right.

It pointed down toward the ground and up into the sky.

The Number 7 was responding to Marlon's every move.

"HAHA! That's it, Marlon," hollered Grandpa McDoogle. "Now swing 'er due west!"

"Yes sir," replied Marlon as he turned the train toward the valley.

At that very moment, Santa was leaving the last house on his route.

A golden cloud swirled up into the smokestack.

Santa had returned.

He looked out of the window at the ground far below.

"Well . . ." said Santa with hesitation. "This is different."

"Welcome back, Mr. Claus!" said Marlon while focusing on flying the train. "Where to next?"

Santa looked at him and smiled a broad smile.

"All the stockings are stuffed.
All the presents are placed.
So back to Hill City
With maximum haste!"

"Back to Hill City! Yes, Sir!" Marlon said as he gave his scarf a powerful tug and the train swung around.

Suddenly, the train began to shake and shudder as the golden steam started to fade.

"AH!" hollered Grandpa McDoogle. "We're running out of magical steam!"

Marlon peered from the cabin to see the train tracks curving down a steep hill below.

"How are you going to get this iron giant back on the track?" Grandpa worried aloud. "If we don't hit the rails straight on, we'll jump the track and CRASH THE WHOLE TRAIN!"

Marlon thought a deep thought and grinned a smart grin.

"Hold on everybody. This will be one heck of a ride!"

Home Again Home Home

Chapter4
Home Again Home

**M**arlon cracked the scarf to the right and levers leaned.

He whipped the scarf to the left and spinners spun.

With a loud creak and a labored chug, the train began a climb straight up toward the stars.

"BOY! YOU'VE LOST YOUR LAST MARBLE! WE NEED TO GO DOWN AND YOU'RE GOING STRAIGHT UP!!" warned Grandpa McDoogle.

"Not for long," Marlon replied.

And he was right.

The Number 7 barreled back toward the ground, and each train car followed closely behind.

The locomotive came so close to the caboose Santa could almost touch it.

Conductors Pemberton, Mills, and Harold the Goon waved confused waves as the caboose continued on the same trip toward the stars that the locomotive had taken moments before.

Marlon focused intensely as he lined
the train up with the track.

With sweat on his brow and hope
in his heart, Marlon pulled the scarf
back one last time.

The boiler howled as the last of the
golden steam was released.

And the locomotive dropped from
the sky.

Sparks flew from the wheels as the
Number 7 hit the track straight on.

Each and every car followed
right behind.

The entire station crew rushed toward the train as it rolled to a stop.

They were astonished (and more than a little relieved) to see the Number 7 return home in one piece.

The reindeer marched to Santa's sleigh in perfect order.

Golden sparks erupted beneath their hooves.

Santa swung down from the locomotive, and his clothes magically changed back.

He walked in large strides toward his sleigh.

Marlon followed cautiously behind. He wasn't sure what everyone would think of his having just flown the town's prized train.

This seems like just the sort of thing that could get a kid grounded for life, Marlon thought.

Santa climbed into his sleigh and looked down at Marlon.

After a moment's silence he began to speak.

"In all of my many,
Many long days,
I've met all sorts of children
With curious ways.

"And I've known around the world
A great trainsman or two,
But a boy who flies trains?
I know only you.

Let's meet here next year,
And for years down the road.
Like your Grandpa before you,
Our secret you'll hold."

Santa smiled a slight smile and winked a slight wink.

"Welcome to the team, Marlon."

"But Santa," Marlon said. "I'm only a kid."

"Well that's your choice to make, isn't it Marlon?" Santa replied.

"After all, I'd be nothing more than a very old man with a very white beard if that's all I wanted to be."

"But, I choose to be something more."

Santa removed his hat and tossed it high into the air.

It transformed into an Engineer's cap and landed softly on Marlon's head.

"A Christmas Eve present, Marlon. Something special, just for you."

"Thank you, Santa," replied Marlon as he took off the hat, "but I can't accept this.

"The whole night has been the most special present I could ever imagine.

"I got to meet you, have an adventure with my grandpa, and I was given the neatest gift anyone could ask for."

Marlon handed the hat back to Santa and proudly cinched his scarf around his neck.

"This gift is far better than any other present could ever be," Marlon said. "I don't need anything else."

"You are truly one of a kind, young man," said Santa in reply.

Santa lifted the reins high, and the reindeer stood at attention.

"Until next year, my friends," Santa said as he brought the reins down.

The sleigh rocketed off, as the sound of sleigh bells faded into the distance.

The snow began to fall again.

The wind began to blow again.

And the train station clock began to tick and tock once more.

Marlon turned to discover that a crowd had gathered around him.

Everyone stood looking at Marlon, silent and still.

Grandpa McDoogle was the first to move.

He slowly removed his hat and gave Marlon a nod of respect.

All across the train yard, each person followed.

Some removed their hats.

Others gave a salute.

And the ladies gave a slight curtsy.

It was a simple, dusty welcome to The Boy Who Flies Trains.

An Exceptional Dream

Chapter 5
An Exceptional Dream

**M**arlon woke on Christmas morning surprised to find that he was lying on the couch in front of the living room window.

He looked to the door where his coat hung neatly on a hook. The long red scarf was nowhere to be seen.

Did I fall asleep in the truck? Marlon wondered.

Or, he was afraid to think, *was it all just a dream?*

Marlon looked out the front window at a blanket of fresh-fallen snow.

No tire tracks could be seen for miles.

"Oh well," he said to himself. "If it had to be a dream, at least it was a great dream."

In the distance, he could see the faces of Mount Rushmore.

Marlon had seen those stone faces 100 times before. But this morning, he thought, they looked particularly sad.

Marlon was grateful for the gifts he received that Christmas – even the sweater he didn't really like but tried on anyway just to be nice.

Marlon realized he was no longer thinking about the toy train that had filled his wishes for so many years.

There was a warm feeling in his heart where that longing used to be. It was a feeling made up of memories from his Christmas Eve adventure with Grandpa McDoogle.

Marlon now knew that memories with family were far more fantastic than any material thing could ever be.

If only it were real, Marlon thought.

Marlon was cleaning up wrapping paper when he heard a knock at the door.

He opened the door and his heart skipped a beat. There stood Grandpa McDoogle holding a long, dusty red scarf. "You left this in the truck last night, lad," he said with a smirk. "I trust you'll take better care of it in the future."

"You bet, Grandpa," Marlon replied. "Most folks might not recognize that such a simple thing can hold a world of adventure!"

"Yes indeed," Grandpa McDoogle said with a wink before turning toward his truck.

He paused and looked back. "Almost forgot. A friend of ours thought you might like a little something else. You should take one last look under the tree."

With that, Grandpa McDoogle hopped into his truck and clamored down the road.

75

Marlon turned back toward the Christmas tree and his eyes widened.

Sitting beneath the branches, where there had been nothing moments before, was a simple package wrapped in brown paper with a scroll tied to the top.

Marlon unrolled the scroll to find
a note addressed to him.

"Young Master McDoogle,

"The Boy Who Flies Trains
Is now part of our team,
Sailing trains through the sky
On magical steam.

"Your landing was rough though,
I think you'd agree.
But for a first flight,
It was alright by me.

"Now please take this gift,
From the reindeer and I,
Because practice makes perfect
When learning to fly.

"Your true friend,

- St. Nicholas Claus."

Marlon carefully untied the bow.

Marlon gently unwrapped the paper.

Marlon slowly lifted the lid off of
the box.

There, before him, was a model train.

It was a perfect replica of the Number
7 with each one of the train cars.

A wooden chest filled the space in
the case where the track would
normally go.

Marlon lifted the chest and slowly opened the lid.

A golden glow filled the room.

"What is that?" asked Marlon's mother as she looked into the room.

"It's magical hay that makes reindeer fly and can send a full-sized steam train up into the sky like Grandpa and I did last night to help Santa Claus fill Christmas stockings while his reindeer refilled their bellies and stoked their fires for the rest of the trip around the world to deliver all the presents!" Marlon gushed.

"Oh, Marlon," dismissed his mother as she walked toward the kitchen. "You've got to stop hanging around Grandpa McDoogle. All that time on trains has made him a bit batty, and it's going to make you a bit batty as well..."

I hope so, Marlon thought. *I hope so indeed.*

That night, after everyone had gone to bed, Marlon placed a small piece of sparkling hay into the model Number 7.

It lifted into the air, and Marlon began to fly it all around the room.

He was practicing for the next Christmas Eve, and for each and every Christmas Eve thereafter.

Marlon McDoogle was a
12-year-old boy.

But on a crisp Christmas Day, not
so very long ago, a 12-year-old boy
wasn't all he wanted to be.

Marlon McDoogle chose to be
something more.

The End

ON A BRISK WINTER DAY

in 2012 Meg Warder, President of Black Hills Central Railroad, challenged Sean Covel with writing a fresh holiday train story using the Black Hills Central Railroad as the inspiration. The Black Hills Central's Engine #7, rolling stock and train station were used as stimulus for the background images in the book all are located in the beautiful Black Hills of South Dakota.

SEAN C. COVEL, WRITER

Sean Covel was raised in the small railroading town of Edgemont, SD, before endeavoring a career in the movie industry. Sean has produced several film and television series including *The 12 Dogs of Christmas* and the iconic independent film, *Napoleon Dynamite*. Sean's book credits include *Marlon McDoogle's Magical Night* and the *Porter the Hoarder* series of look-and-find books. When not writing books or making movies, Sean serves as an Adjunct Professor at the University of Southern California School of Cinematic Arts. He travels often, but hangs his nunchucks in Deadwood, SD.

DIEGO VELASQUEZ, ILLUSTRATOR

Diego Velasquez is an illustrator, visual developer and conceptual artist. Diego started his career as a children's book illustrator before transitioning to the world of blockbuster movies. Diego has worked as a concept artist on several large Hollywood movies including *Aquaman, Guardians of the Galaxy 2, Tomb Raider, Justice League* and *Black Panther*. Diego was born in Santander, Colombia, and holds a Master's Degree in Animation and Visual Effects from the Academy of Art University in San Francisico, CA.

First edition, 2019
Copyright 2019 by Baby Buddha, LLC

Graphic Design - Brett Wingate

ISBN 978-1-7323681-0-1

BABY BUDDHA
PUBLISHING

To visit the real life Engine Number 7 and ride the 1880 Train, make reservations at www.1880train.com